THE

C000052068

CHESTER

Barbara Maitra

(A Collection of Short Stories)

CSP

Canaan-Star Publishing

First published by Canaan-Star Publishing, United Kingdom in (2024)

A Catalogue record for this book is available from the British Library.

ISBN: 978-1-909484-50-4

Book cover design by Mubbashir Hayat

Dedication

This story is dedicated to my wonderful family members at home, abroad and extended xx

Other Books by Barbara Maitra

Chasing Shadows
(2023)

The Spice Years
(2022)

We Came to a River
(2013)

The Perversity of Diamonds
(2013)

The Girl Who Went Back
(2013)

—

Content

THE CHARA
TO
CHESTER

(A Collection of Short Stories)

Barbara Maitra

1

GROWING UP

There were just the two of us alighting from the 8.40 and waiting for the Milton Keynes connection. After drifting around in the morning sunshine and weighing each other up the announcement came confirming that our train was delayed for an hour. We exchanged glances of dismay and looked around for a bench but spotted a retiring room: long retired judging by its forlorn, unpainted look. And we headed inside.

For some time, there was silence broken by the young lady.

'What do you think has happened?'

'Could be serious, or not.' I replied. 'I read that there is at least one fatal incident on the railways every day or maybe the driver hasn't turned up. Their wives have babies and things.'

'Oh dear.' Was the response followed by deeper

silence.

The young lady was one of the prettiest, no, one of the most beautiful girls I had seen. She had copper coloured hair, the most enormous blue eyes, the deep blue of my garden Lythodermas and a porcelain skin. She looked elegant in a plain powder blue dress, its only ornament, three miniature self-covered buttons on a flared sleeve. She carried a leather shoulder bag and I saw a plain band on her ring finger. She looked at her watch frequently and I felt bound to break the silence this time.

'It won't come any quicker clock watching. Have you an appointment somewhere.'

'I have,' she answered, 'but I'm just an impatient kind of person.'

'Well, I do have an appointment. I'm Mrs Bland by the way – you are Mrs?'

'Oh no,' was the hasty response. She looked at her ring, 'Divorced, couldn't get it off.'

I could not resist,

'You don't look old enough to be married, never mind divorced?'

'Things go wrong don't they. Are you married?'

'I was, for over fifty years. My husband died.'

'How sad and how lovely,' she added, 'Just like my mum and dad.'

I am usually right about people. I could sense she was not shy of divulging anything personal. I suppose it has to do with speaking to someone as old as I am, like a big sponge who has absorbed so much in life that nothing can shock. I was right.

'Yes, I should have seen it coming. It was a bad match. He was way out of my league.'

I felt like asking her if she had looked in the mirror recently. With her looks she could have married a prince.

'Did you meet at a polo match or something?' It was the classiest venue that came to mind. What a clumsy joke. But she saw the point, smiled and replied, 'in the hairdressers. I was a hairdresser. The place was "posh" she added with a smiling reference to the "polo joke" 'and this bloke came regularly. He always had beautiful suits with white shirts and clean collars. You notice collars as a hairdresser. He was a cut above the others.' She laughed then, 'Sorry about that. He never sat to me, but you know when a feller fancies you, kept looking and more looking then one day asked me out for a date.'

'It sounds like a fairy-tale romance starting.' I prompted.

'Yes, it does. The wedding should have been a warning I suppose. Against my suggestion the invites went out too late for most of my clan to attend. They were mostly Gustav's family and friends.' She saw my eyebrows raised at the unusual name. 'No, he wasn't called Gustav, but he owns the big estate agents in the town, and you might know him. That's not fair.'

'Why, what did he do, or not do.?

'After the wedding I felt like he was training me, a bit like a dog. When he called people to dinner – not my friends – we went through the table routine, where to put what and when to serve this and that. Gustav, I told him, I wasn't dragged up, we ate with knives and forks, and we even had napkins at Christmas.' *Darling Emma, you're so young and I'm so fussy* was his reply but he spoiled it by saying *you're learning.*'

'We had a few run-ins like that. It really was like animal training till I did things his way. Sit down, stand up beg, but they started to get serious. Am I talking too much?' she asked.

'No, no it's so interesting. Not because it ends badly - as you say – in divorce but we all learn something about others in these exchanges. Do I sound stuffy?' She laughed and carried on.

'Well, we've a lot of time to kill. It got serious over the red dress to the Rotary club dinner. *Buy yourself something nice for the outing, it's important to me.*' he said. There was a pause whilst we exchanged looks, 'Yes, he controlled the finance, so off I went and bought a green outfit. I saw one of those oldie films with a star in it with my colouring.'

'Maureen O'Hara' I interjected. I knew she'd reminded me of someone.

'That's the one,' came back at me. 'She wore a lot of green and looked gorgeous. I presented myself all ready to go. He shook his head, *Dear Emma I meant one like the red dress I bought you last month, that's got class and women notice these things. Off you go and change.* I was furious. I told him that red made me look like a tart with this colour hair. Another put down, *Emma trust me, they're my sort. You'll come to understand.*'

'Oh dear, I can see where this is leading. Why did you stay with him?' Unabashed she came out with,

'The sex was magnifico and I sort of knew I did not fit into his world completely and that I should try. The sex devoured me.' She paused for a moment then added,' But then sex is sex. You can have that with anyone. Love needn't come into it.' She sounded as if she had just made that discovery in this moment.

'Sex is important,' I added feebly.

'Hmm,' she continued. 'I suppose I started to recognise what Gustav was doing. I'm a slow learner it seems. He was starting to dominate. I was being bullied.'

'How can you do that in this day and age?' I asked knowing without details that relationships do get unbalanced. If one agrees to be bullied the other gets away with murder. I do mean murder also. The bullied snap eventually, don't they?

'The pegs were serious.'

'Pegs?'

'Yes, little plasticky things did it. When it was fine, I liked to hang the washing out on the line: bypass the drier. Well, he came home from work and couldn't take his eyes off the washing line. *What's this. Our private life out there for everyone to see?* Gustav, everyone wears knickers and knows you wear boxers. What's wrong? *Wrong* was an obsession with the pegging. *If we have a vulgar line up, WE (*he meant me of course) *should match blue to blue, red to red not the* *don't care line up you have here. Don't do it again.'*

'I can hardly believe a man would say that. Didn't your friends put you right about behaviour: sort of talking about their own blokes?'

'I didn't have any friends after two years of this. But I did answer back. *Gustav this is weird, I think you need help.* When I looked at him, he was stiff with fury. I'm not kidding. The washing line did that to him. I was getting a bit scared by now and only half defied Gustav by hanging the washing out again. This time I matched the red peg to my red bra, the blue one to his blue socks, the green to my lovely dress. I've done it your way I said when he came home. *I won't repeat myself, last warning.* he said. I was so upset I spoke to my mother about him properly this time. Mum was quite cute after all, asking me how things were, and I'd answered "fine" for ages.

I crossed my fingers. 'And what did she advise?'

'I knew something wasn't right. Be careful. Don't provoke him. You have to work something out properly with a man like that. You've waited for two years, hold on a bit longer.'

She burst out laughing. 'Well, I told you I was impatient. I went back and did the exact opposite full-on mismatching. My way. When he saw the line, he stood rigid, his face was almost purple. *You defied me, Emma. I need to teach you to listen.* And he slapped me hard. That was the last thing he did. I packed all my stuff, except the red dress, and went back to mum and dad. Despite her advice I think mum expected me. She'd made my bed up.'

'Wow, that's quite a story. And where are you going to today. You look lovely by the way. Is it special?'

The announcement came over the Tanoy clearly informing us that the train for Milton Keynes would arrive at our platform within two minutes. We both got up from the hard wooden seats.

'Yes, I'm meeting Josh the new boyfriend. Do you think he'll like this dress? I don't want to make any more mistakes, so I asked him his favourite colour.'

My heart sank, my thoughts were, *here we go again.*

'And what is it. What's his favourite colour?'

'Yellow,' she replied raising her arm with the powder blue frill, in a gesture of goodbye. As I followed her to the exit, I saw the back of the elegant dress for the first time. It was beautifully finished with a row of self-covered tiny buttons from neck to waist.

It looked like a backbone.

2

A ROBOTIC FUTURE

That wasn't supposed to happen.

Number 14 and 17, two robots had fought and dismantled each other. Plastic and metal functions had been reduced to the bits that lay down there in the crater. Bruce was shocked but wasn't surprised. He'd had the dream again last night. The one that signalled disaster. He had bought that house again. The one that teetered on the edge of wasteland. As usual, he had entered through the front door and then been trapped in a maze of windowless rooms: rooms up, down and through with no exit. Whenever the dream visited him, he knew something would threaten the following day. And here it was – wreckage.

His assistant Joe was first with his opinion, 'I reckon that's a Friday afternoon job. They didn't tighten the screws.'

He was probably right. Bruce wanted to believe

that, but the dream was a warning. It always was. Was worse to follow? Bruce was looking down from a high ridge to the quarry where he was in control. 'I hate those guys.'

His undermanager Joe, joined in 'Yeah. Fucking Frankinsteins'.

'Give me the old days when you could use real people, prison labour. This lot freaks me out.' Bruce took a quick survey of the workforce below. 'Joe, call the spooks. We forgot to report Number 27 yesterday. Remember? he refused the order to 'lift'.'

'Shall we really spook the spooks and tell them 29 was picking his nose?'

'Get out of here Joe. I'm not joking and I'm not happy'.

This was robot world, the world they inhabited now. A series of pandemics following Sars and Mers had decimated humans. Sars and Mers were scary because they killed instantly but, in that act, destroyed their breeding ground and themselves. The series of pandemics which followed were run by more evil viruses. Bruce called them 'thinking' viruses. They had worked out the theory of replicating, killing the host slowly and inexorably, along the way, leaving enough meat to carry on hosting themselves. And steadily they were wiping out the whole human race.

Paperbacks were still around as Bruce grew up: shiny-fronted, illustrated. He never forgot the hero who discovered an Eldorado but was chased away by an army of red worms crawling en masse to devour him as he made for his refuge. His plane took off as one reached his left boot. Worms? Virus? interchangeable horrors.

He looked down on the bobbing heads, helmeted, looking like billiard balls on a sandy table. They leaned forward, backwards and upwards with the digging and lifting. This scene represented progress: a way of creating manpower lost to pandemics. But it had its alarm worries: all that energy harnessed to grunt jobs, digging, pushing, crushing. In Bruce's opinion it was the purple nightmare of a group of MP's drunk on technology. Bruce's fear that these were not just machines gave them a scare factor like the thinking viruses, the red worms of childhood stories. Cynically he wondered how many men living in gated compounds had grown rich on contracts for Robotics. A campaign had made the public embrace them. Even his own wife, against his objections, had ordered a Pollymaid who served perfect tea, cleaned floors and sanitised the toilets. It was not right and not a happy solution.

Bruce noticed the slowing movement of 21 and 22. He blew his supersonic whistle and shouted 'fillup'. Both bots dropped their load of ten-ton rocks and made for the crater rim where the chargers were. They swivelled to access the machine and plugged themselves in. Joe called out, 'OK Brucie they'll be fixed in an hour then back on the floor again.'

They were undeniably clever robots. For Bruce who was a 'man' manager it had been a steep learning curve emotionally to switch to Sappies: the robots' collective name. They responded to voice commands that were simple grunt orders for grunt jobs: *Lift, drop, forward, backward, halt*. His worries, which kept him awake at night, came after number 33 had malfunctioned. The Spooks had come down from Berrybridge and removed its hard drive. They had collapsed with laughter.

'My god those kids in Birmingham need a thrashing'.

'What's up?' Bruce had muscled in on a discussion from which he felt excluded.

'They've programmed it in Latvian.'

'Why?'

'Just messing. They think it's funny'. Bruce had felt his blood pressure rise.

'Why?' He repeated. Then panic kicked in, *what else had they done?*

The spooks looked at him. 'It's the only fun they get I suppose. And they are just kids. They've fulfilled their brief and created replacements for human beings'.

'I hated these things before we met. I'm **afraid**

of them now I know kids are *messing.*'

The spooks whose correct name was *fixers* had shaken their heads.

'We get it. And we told the government not to hand out contracts till the firms had been vetted. But who listens to scientists? I suppose the generation of IT kids had to have jobs, their destiny to fill the lost labour market'.

'Maybe those kids should pop down here one day and see what one of their creations can really do. A ten-ton rock on their keyboard fingers would sort them out'. Bruce was furious and remained wary. So here they were again looking at 27's refusal to 'lift'. The fixers' brows were still knitted as they wrestled with an explanation for the disobedience. 'Was Joe eating a sandwich or something when he gave the order?' the fixers asked. 'They are sensitive to language commands and maybe it was muffled. We can't see any reason for non-compliance'. But, in the end the fixer remained perplexed, they completed the paperwork and hauled 27 into their trailer.

'Let me know the outcome', Bruce called after them. 'I need to know what I'm up against here'.

His sleep was disturbed that night, haunted with *what ifs.* Clever, wet-behind the-ears-kids, in charge, worried Bruce. He had a different skill set to robot handling. He had commanded men in three wars and raised a family, threading a perilous way through this new robotic world in which he had no trust. Eventually he gave in, turned over and pulled the sheet over his head to hide the dawn.

By midday Joe and Bruce were down in the shallow crater awaiting Barney with his dumpster truck. It would take only an hour for the *Sappies* to load the 260 tons. He could see the arithmetic and appreciate the results, but his gut reaction was anxiety. It was almost like having a disease where you were not fully in control, hence the unease. Maybe he was becoming paranoid, but he had caught number 44 looking at him when he spoke. 44 had three eyes to every other machine's two. His 3 eyes glowered rather than glowed. Bruce shook his head. *If I'm to stick this job and survive this new world I'd better put a stop to these thoughts or quit.*

Barney's bright orange dumpster arrived in a swirl of dust.

'Barney. Late again.' Bruce called but he was always pleased to see him. He represented real people.

'Sorry guys. Had to stop for repairs. Tyre hit a fork in the road.'

'That one must be out of a cracker Barney. Terrible.'

'That's my reward for bringing a bit of sunshine into your lives down here. I'll stop trying.'

Barney jumped down from the dumpster: always good for a laugh. He reminded Bruce of his father. He was calling out, 'Latest news - Did you know Jimmy has married a Popsie?'

'What's a Popsie?'

'One of those upmarket Bot brides. All frilly

knickers, long legs, blonde.'

'Unbelievable', Bruce replied. '

'Know why they're called Popsie?'

'I'm not interested but you're going to tell me Barney.'

'Well, hell no. You think about it.'

'Now you've got that off your chest what's the load demand for next week?'

Barney consulted his logbook then paused, sometimes he was unstoppable, 'Have you heard this one guys, it'll kill you?

Before he could continue, 44, the three-eyed Sappy raised its arm, picked up a rock and heaved it. Bruce watched its journey in slow motion. His ex-army skills calculated the projectile's mission from launch to target and realised there was not a thing he could do about it. It landed on Barney's head and Barney's arm with the *mother* Tattoo landed at Bruce's feet as an intestine draped a rock, like a livid snake. But it was the mush of Barney's brains within a splintered skull which upset Bruce. Two seconds ago, this was an entertaining human being with feeling, reduced to nothing by the soulless thing standing over him. Bruce had seen war and death but that was all behind him and had had a purpose. This shocked and frightened him. The three - eyed Sappy stood immobile and Bruce knew with a tingle, right down to his coccyx, that it was glaring. He was afraid to give a command. He whispered to Joe to follow him to the office and was aware of the three-eyed Sappy stare following their movements.

Work halted for the day. Uncertainty hung over them like a threat. Bruce was calling the fixers.

'Get over here, now. There's a psychopath among your programmers and the three eyed Sappy has pulped my dump truck driver. His guts are spread all over the rocks'. *That should bring them running, and it did.*

Fixers stared in disbelief at the mess. When they opened their mouths to speak Bruce held his finger to his lips and signalled them 'inside'.

'Be careful what you say. I don't know what command triggered that action. Which lab produced the three-eyed Sappy. The jokers in Birmingham again?'

'No.' the Fixer was sure. He consulted a red, bound notebook, 'That would be Edinburgh,' He took some time to read the page in front of him, 'Oh my god,' he spluttered, 'I remember that lab. They took on some psychiatric patients from the local treatment centre. They had majored in programming and were given a new start in life'. He rustled through his notes again, 'Definitely, Edinburgh. We warned about vetting, now some monster has slipped through the mesh: smart but psychopathic, as you say'. They turned to look at Sappy 44 who seemed alert, waiting for something. Bruce shivered: *another kill command behind those buttons and screens.*

Let's get on with something we know they'll do without any problem,' Bruce said. He lifted his version of a megaphone and called *Lift*. The Sappies including the three eyed killer animated their arms cum jaws, each lifted their 10 tons of rock and stood. Then a commanding voice which sounded inhumanly sinister because it truly was inhuman, boomed - LOOK AT ME. Bruce was wide eyed with disbelief and a dawning horror that this move was new and threatening. 'They're not programmed to speak, are they?'

What came next was more frightening. The three-eyed Sappy bellowed the word FOLLOW and they all lined up behind him as he marched forward. None of the commands formerly used by Bruce and his team were working. *Stand. Still. Stop,* had no effect. The march moved forward with all the fixation of driver ants, unstoppable.

'Fucking Frankinsteins are making for the village.' Joe called.

'Get the nearest lab to zap them,' ordered Bruce, 'a lightning strike took out the grid last week that should do it. God help us'.

They could hear it now. The onward march of metallic feet pounding the tarmac carrying 300 tons of rock. Police helicopters were out adding urgency to the ominous sounds. In ten minutes, Bruce calculated they would reach the village. The village school was first. He looked down at the mess that had been Barney. He leaned forwards, head in his hands. It seems the only thing that brought about his death were the friendly words, 'This joke'll kill you.'

He turned on the TV in the absence of any other information. It graphically recorded the systematic decimation of buildings, cars and people. Already, habitation had been reduced to a parking lot. The TV recorded an onward march to the National grid which Bruce calculated might stop them. Or would it?

This was the world we had built now being rapidly unbuilt he thought. And in a twisted way, he saw the justice of it all.

Barbara Maitra

3

ANGEL DUST

They were dressing the tree and Freddie had the angel in his hand, ready for the top branches.

'Freddie you're only 5 and not going up there without the proper steps. They've a screw loose and jammed so Dad's going to fix them and first thing tomorrow……

'That's right son. Get yourself off to bed now, I'll have the steps fixed and Bob's your uncle.'

'Dad, Bobs not my uncle it's Simon,' Freddie said gruffly.

'Yep, spot on. Now, step into your jamas, up we go and in we go. Sleep well.'

Freddie was disappointed, but he'd gone past his bedtime doing the tree and was very tired, so he fell asleep very quickly.

*****

The sound of crying disturbed Freddie. Or was it the cat Marmalade who'd gone walkabout for a whole week and now wanted to be let in? No. He went over to the window. There was an Angel in the garden sitting on the swing: Head in hand, the Angel cried softly.

'What's wrong?' Freddie asked.

'I'm lost,' the Angel replied.

'Well sit for a bit on our garden bench till you remember where you were going.' The angel floated over. 'Dad made the bench. It's nicer with cushions on. But they get wet outside.' The angel stopped crying. Its wings shook displaying shimmering stars mixed in with the trailing feathers.

'Ooh! Do that again,' Freddie said,' some of your sparkles have fallen on the grass.'

'I think it might be a sprinkling of snow.' And the angel shivered its feathers again. Freddie laughed, delighted. A bright moon made the angel's feathers luminous.

'Can you fly?'

'Come on now Freddie: What are these for?' and the angel gave a hop, flapped its wings and hovered over Freddie's head.

'Don't go,' Freddie called.' Sit down and I'll get the cushions for the seat. Make you more comfortable.'

'I wasn't going anywhere, I'm still lost.' Freddie studied the angel taking in the long hair and glittering shoes. An owl flew over the moon.

'Are you a man or a woman?' Freddie asked.

'Angels aren't anything. Just Angels.'

'Then you could have a haircut with me before Christmas. It's a unisex salon. Your hair IS very long'. The angel shook its head making the curls tinkle.

'You sound like my triangle at school. I'm in Mrs Kerridges orchestra. Have you remembered yet where you were going?'

'Yes almost. I'm guardian angel to Mr Potts'.

'Oh, I know Mr Potts, he's only a few doors

down. Look, he's got a monkey puzzle tree in his garden.' They both looked at the tree twisting away up to the moon. 'Have I got a guardian angel?' Freddie asked.

'We're a bit short at the moment. It's the population explosion, so not enough to give everybody one'.

'Yes, I know. The TV says there are too many people in the world. So have I got one? You didn't say.'

'You share one with Mr Potts, I guess that's why I ended up here. What a muddle.'

'Can I have you for Christmas?'

'I'm afraid Mr Potts has got Christmas booked because he's lonely.' A desolate hoot came from the owl.

'What do you do guardian angel? Was it you stopped me falling in the lake when I walked on the ice last week and it cracked?'

'Well, I stand behind you on your shoulder and

try to steer you into doing good things.'

'Mr Potts doesn't need you like I do. He doesn't play on the ice. He stays in all the time. I guess he won't even come out for Christmas.'

'That's right I'll have to stick around and give him company: Put songs in his head and make him feel happy'.

'Well, if I do all those things for him can I have you for Christmas?'

'What things?'

'Well, I can sing my favourite carol to him.' Freddie's voice soared clear as crystal as the angel folded its wings and listened.

Snowy flakes are falling softly
Clothing all the world in white
High above the stars are shining.
Twinkling through the darkest night.'

'That's very, very good,' the angel said unfolding its wings.

'I can also deliver his cards, that'll make him

feel happy.'

The angel shook its glittering wings. 'I'll think about it', was the reply. Freddie was fascinated every time the angel shook its wings.

'Of course, I've got an angel on my tree, but you are more beautiful.'

The angel's wings trembled as its feet lifted off the ground. 'Just going to check on Mr Potts. I'll be back soon.'

*****

When Freddie came down for breakfast, he saw that Dad had fixed the steps and he went to pick up the angel for the tree.

'Up you go son. Steady on. Put that ring on the top branch and Bob's your uncle.'

'Dad stop saying that. It's not true.'

The post made a loud plop as a pile of Christmas cards came through the letterbox. Mother was opening and reading them: 'Aunty May, still alive and Joe here, lovely picture. He hopes we'll visit him this summer. No chance unless he moves from Reykjavik. Oh, my sister Fanny, off again on a cruise. That woman really can't stand the cold.'

'She can't stand still.' Dad said.

'Well, here's one from Mr Potts. That's nice of him. Look, there's an angel on the front. Really pretty.'

'I know,' Freddie said, 'it's his guardian angel, but I've got him for Christmas.'

'You certainly have,' mother said looking up at the tree.' Doesn't he look special right up there in heaven.'

'Can I take our card round to Mr Potts? I can tell him about his guardian angel. What I tell him will really make him happy.'

'What a nice thought Freddie. He must be lonely in that bungalow all on his own for Christmas. Tell you what, we can do better than that, I'll have a word with Dad about him coming round for dinner. How's that?'

Barbara Maitra

4

JUST A PHONE CALL AWAY

'Killer Romeos don't actually kill, they only cheat.'

Judy recalled Clarissa's words as she eased on her trainers. She sniffed the weather. It was cold and dark out there and a gritty wind stirred the trees. Certainly, a challenge: like getting the rest of that story out of Clarissa. She pushed her foot firmly into the trainers, slung on the safety Day-Glo jacket and her legs were going piston-like up the hill. *Breathe Judy breathe* she admonished and took in a mouthful of autumn mist. Clarissa was waiting for her at the top of the road. Clarissa was not a serious exerciser; the gear was much more dedicated than she was. She looked good in anything even the outfit, clumpy on others, gave her a model figure. The two friends jogged together winding through the estate, bobbing up and down like an incandescent lemon and orange.

'Only going as far as my house then you're on

your own,' Clarissa said. Judy expected that.

'OK. Short and sweet tonight, is it? Ring me if you're coming tomorrow and we'll meet up. By then the weather might have cleared up a bit.'

'Can't ring', she panted. 'Lost my mobile. But I'll be there. That's definite. I've lost three Kilos since I've jogged. I'll be there same time tomorrow. Another couple of pounds to go.' Getting a rhythm to their breathing halted any further conversation. When their lungs were in harmony with their running legs Judy could not resist the question,

'How's it going with Romeo'? She asked. Clarissa always had a 'Romeo' in her sights, and it was always a disastrous but entertaining story.

'Who? Oh, you mean the latest. Well, he's the 'late' Romeo. Nasty experience with that one. Ditched him last week.'

'Do tell!' Judy demanded.

'I will. Just let me get my thoughts together and my breath back. It's a longish story, bit scary also.'

'Internet malfunction?' Judy asked glancing sideways at Clarissa. *Yes, the tension was there. It was something to do with her prowling the internet.* That's where Clarissa had picked up some dodgy characters recently. 'You know it's dangerous, don't you?' Judy resumed. 'They don't call it *Windows* for nothing. Every time you're looking at the screen, little green men are looking back at you.' Clarissa snorted: part derision, part out of breath.

'Steady you're scaring the pants off me,' she said.

'No that's the little green man's job hopefully,' Judy teased.' Or one day it could be the killing fields.'

'Romeos don't kill they only cheat.'

'There you go again. You said that last week. You sound so sure. Don't be.'

'Nah! They're usually married, that's their only fault.' The tension had come back into Clarissa's voice. Judy suspected she was hiding quite a lot behind those flippant remarks. They jogged evenly for a few minutes with no further outpourings from Clarissa until she broke the silence.

'Anyway, enough about me. What about you. Anyone on the horizon?'

'No horizon and certainly no-one even closer than that and beating down my door. Where do you look for nice blokes nowadays,' Judy continued, 'Pubs, clubs, work? Why don't we have Matchmakers like the Jews or the Asians?'

'Look in the Yellow pages.' Clarissa said and they both laughed. Clarissa veered off and almost collapsed at her front door. 'This is where Miss Dynamic lives with her two cats. See you tomorrow.'

'What about your story?'

'Got to think about it, I've written it all down, but it needs some editing actually or I'll just end up with a massive ear bashing from you.'

'You are so annoying,' Judy let fly as Clarissa firmly closed her front door. It successfully closed any further probing from Judy also. Clarissa waved through the window and pulled a face as she drew her curtains. That killed the warm orange glow from her table lamp. Judy took a breather for a moment picturing Clarissa, feet up, glass in hand and cosy. She thought of turning back herself. Such a dreary evening. Judy put that aside and dredged up the effort to carry on. *Breathe Judy Breathe.*

It was always the same exchange with Clarissa: Judy trying to subdue Clarissa's dangerous search for love via internet dating. They were ding dong arguments, just sound and fury: Clarissa never listened, never took advice *Why do I bother*? Judy asked herself. They both shared the need for a relationship, but Judy was never tempted to go down Clarissa's route. *Breathe Judy Breathe* she panted as she left the houses, and her feet met the bypass road. The metalled surface seemed harsher tonight. A car passed and she could see her own shoes lit up like a rainbow. Just as she thought how pretty they looked there was a sudden shrill ring from somewhere and Judy clapped her ears Tinnitus! No, it wasn't her ears; that was a real ring tone. There is something about a phone ringing that impels. Judy was almost frantic to find and silence it. With sudden co-ordination of eye, ear and hand she dived into the sedge disturbing the faint methane smell which comes from rotting vegetation and a slim silver mobile was in her hand vibrating. She lifted the cover. A voice like no other was whispering in her ear. If voices had colour this would be black and velvet.

'You're still running.' *Wow!* She thought. *How does he know*? And she wanted to hear that voice again.

'Yep!' She replied and waited.

'I'll wait for you under the station clock again tonight. Come back.' Her head was a beehive suddenly with a million messages buzzing. It was such a seductive voice. She found the idea of meeting under the station clock very attractive. She was on the verge of a naughty giggle. Doubtless these errant thoughts were the result of listening to Clarissa's twittering about mating with the unknown. But the voice was undeniably seductive.

Silently she savoured it.

'Are you still there?' She gave a grunt.

'This is the third call and you never answered one of them.' *Yes, because I've only just met you, toffee voice. I wonder what you look like.*

'Where are you exactly?' the voice came back and involuntarily it came out,

'Cedar Avenue.' There was a pause. He hadn't caught on yet that she wasn't the phone owner. Good, she'd hear the voice again. It was delicious having this proxy lover. The naughty giggle rose in her throat again.

'Cedar, where I left you,' he murmured, 'So you're feeling sorry about last night?' he questioned. Again, she replied in universal grunt language.

'Yea'. A pause followed which seemed tactile it was so heavy,

'Cedar, that's where you left me yesterday in the layby. I'm coming to get you this time. No more running Clarissa. *So, it **was** Clarissa's phone in her hand.* You've got to hear my side of the story. I didn't kill her you know.'

Judy froze. There was an iron fist behind the velvet voice that now stunned her. Horror was in her voice as her, 'What!' exploded down the phone. She could visualise the punch that landed from his sharp intake of breath: He now knew he was not speaking to the girl who owned the phone.

'Who are you?' eventually came like an accusation. She was nervous. She had told this stranger, Clarissa's pickup who used the word KILL in his conversation, where she was! Cedar Avenue was a long lonely one. Where would the seeker come from? He said he was at the station. Which direction was the station? He would come from that way. She turned her head. No, he would approach from over there. Her brain was like a blancmange, she couldn't even recall the route she ran so often. Where was the layby? A car passed lighting her Day-Glo up like a beacon, it made her a target. A faint buzz came from the phone in her hand, and she flicked the switch. *Chuck the jacket!* was her gut reaction? 'No,' she decided, turning it inside out. That took care of the target but what about the shoes? *Keep them*, she decided - no matter they winked at every step, they were the lifeline back to safety. Terror and fury with Clarissa took over. She had to make it home before his car came. *Breathe Judy Breathe.* She felt for the phone, fumbling, not remembering the jacket was inside out. Finding the pocket at last she felt the phone. *What an idiot I am I have a phone with me. H*er fingers seemed to have swelled to twice their size as she tapped out 999. The phone lit up then died: battery gone. Now it was *run Judy run, breathe Judy run faster and make for the woods*. She launched herself into a tangle of brambles as car headlights fanned the distant undergrowth. She lay still. The car halted. That must be the layby ahead: That wonderful, terrifying voice drifted through the trees,

'Girl! Whoever you are come out. I must explain.' There was a profound silence whilst Judy breathed, an owl hooted, and something ran up her leg.

'Girl, listen', the soft voice crept down her spine

where tension paralysed her. Interminable silence: A nettle was stinging a part of her neck: It was agony to restrain her hand from pushing it aside. She lay there listening, rigid with tension. He was listening also. A dog barked. *Maybe someone walking their dog* she thought and almost welcomed the snuffle of an animal sniffing her out with a friendly owner at the end of a lead. She waited. If Black Velvet Voice pressed deeper into the undergrowth she would surely be spotted. Something was wriggling in her ear, and she was helpless to investigate. Then she heard the startup sound of an engine. She remained motionless however, alert to any danger. *He might have started the car as a decoy tactic, and I haven't heard him move off yet.*

The wind rose higher, rattling the seed heads of summer-dried plants. Judy strained to clear all but what she needed to hear. Relief swept through her as she heard the buzz of the engine fade into a low growl as it reached the road end. She lay for another half hour breathing in fern and nettle before she felt it safe to move off. She was stiff, sore and scratched and the nettles had stung more than her neck. She pulled a dried leaf from the ear that had wriggled then made for home and Clarissa. She hammered on Clarissa's door. It was opened by Clarissa in a towel gown and smelling of the Moringa hair shampoo she used.

'Didn't know you'd be back so soon. I've just finished writing up the report. It tells you everything.' She joked. 'Come in.' Then she looked closely at Judy. 'Never mind *come in*, you look *all in*. What's happened. Did you get lost in the woods?' Judy stepped inside.

'Talking of lost,' she said holding out her hand, 'This is yours.' The slim silver phone shone brighter reflecting the indoor lights. Except in the business of boyfriends Clarissa was quite bright and Judy watched dawning comprehension flicker across her face. 'I've heard the story now that you didn't tell.' Judy continued. 'You can scrap the report. You want advice? Hand this over to the police and let them find him before he finds you.'

Barbara Maitra

5

RED RETOLD

She donned her red cloak and picked up the basket. It was heavy with the contents. She had included the axe even though it weighed the wicker carrier down to her ankles encased in matching red boots. She took a last look around, closed the door and set off for the woods. Freedom at last. She was not at all sad at what she had done. In fact, she had rather enjoyed it.

There were a few wolves roaming around. The main pack controlled by her grandmother was circling but she was prepared. From time to time, she fed the path with bits of meat which kept them at bay.

The lights of the cottage glowed yellow through the birch trees. Jonas the woodcutter had the fire going and she speeded up anxious to share the warmth. She hammered on the door hoping Jonas would come quickly. All the meat in the basket was finished, a wolf almost nipping her heels. She laid the basket down and lifted the iron latch herself.

No wonder Jonas hadn't heard her. He was in bed. He lifted his head and peered through the heavy black waves of hair which fell about his face, startled at seeing her.

'How did you get away. I didn't think you were coming,' he said keeping the blankets up to his chin.

'Well, you can get up now I have some supper for us.' She turned aside to put the basket out of the way and warm herself beside the glowing logs in the grate. There was no movement from Jonas so, keeping beside the warmth of the fire she fixed her attention on the bed.

'Have you put on weight since last month. You look so big?'

'It's just the blankets make me look twice my size.' The cover slipped from his shoulders revealing the hairs on his chest and a little further. She was intrigued.

'I see you're sleeping without your britches. You never do that in winter?'

'You should try it,' he said, 'it's an experience.

Now go and change your cloak in the scullery. It's all wet. Is it raining outside?

She looked down at the hem where the blood had turned the red cloak maroon. 'Stop messing about and get up.' She ordered. 'I'll change it later.' With that he pushed the covers aside and she could see his magnificent body: Truly naked.

'What's the lump in the bed there?'

'As you said, my britches'. He got up and came forward, hands on her shoulders, steering her towards the scullery.

'Well, I'm not getting into bed with mucky working togs.' With that she broke loose and stepping towards the bed thrust the remaining covers aside. She saw the miller's daughter lying there her yellow hair spread over the sheepskin pillow.

She swivelled swiftly picking up the axe from the basket. She got to work just as she had on her grandmother.

Barbara Maitra

6

THE CHARA TO CHESTER

I organised a trip from our village in the Wirral. We're all friends & going to Chester.

Everything ticketiboo, seats allotted and circulated.

Came the day.

Sally won't sit with John because she's wearing her best but come prepared for the worst. So, the backup outfits need a whole seat: plastic mac, headgear, scarves, galoshes, fur coat, suntan lotion, shades and a golf brolly. I'd like to ask her **where** she thinks she's going but as we're all friends I remain polite.

Just stow the animal in the rack above your head I say. (her fur coat)

And Betty now wants the seat next to Joe - her brother. She hasn't spoken to him since he was 10 but apparently taken charge since his wife died.

I'm standing helpless with the clipboard whilst musical

chairs go on, nobody is where I put them.

All we need is the music. Then Darling Gabriel gives up his seat to Displaced John and we're sorted.

Basically - we're all great friends in the Wirral.

Gilda rolls up dressed like a diva in violet chiffon.

Nothing warm and not much underneath as we all see when she passes through sunshine.

I never knew she had such sturdy legs.

Halfway to Chester, without warning, she breaks into song.

Exhilaration of the autumn morning glowing through the Wirral?

Who Knows?

She's got no voice and obviously never heard herself sing.

She's having a go at Molly Malone and fumbles the words.

This is too much for the back row who are all left wing anyway.

Give us a break Gilda whilst you figure out whether it was cockles, mussels, Dublin or Belfast.

And the chant goes up WE WANT TO KNOW, with clapping.

Tension rises for a moment. Then it slackens as underneath

we're all friends from our village.

Fred has boarded laden with nets.

He has two seats to himself because of the jars, the booklets, the samples an' all.

He's fixated on the common house fly. It's his hobby.

And sometimes he acts like one.

He's buzzing up and down the bus telling anyone who will listen:

Let me get this right - about the 2 eyes on the fly's head with 100s of hexagonal lenses and 3 smaller eyes in between.

He's fizzing with a fly's dynamic energy.

Swat him comes from the Lefties in the back and again

half the bus laugh but you can smell it -intolerance is rising.

Thank goodness Fred wearies and sits with his nose against the window, His black moustache just like a squashed fly.

I did hesitate,

But then he's part of the community

And in our village in the Wirral - we're all friends.

For the record - Miriam is stalking me with her notebook.

She thinks I haven't noticed.

The next committee meeting will be lively.

Gordon. the muddy gardener, has devised a quiz to pass the time and comes up front.

He's unrecognisable today in a smart jacket with a red bow tie: very much the question Master.

His love is gardening, and he knows why some rhododendrons are pink and some blue.

Things like that.

Unfortunately, *notebook Miriam* is a teacher, knows everything and wont bend.

She's challenging the definition of hardwood and softwood trees.

I smell it again - Irritation is rising, everyone shuffling in their seats as if they'd been sanded.

Luckily Gabriel was on hand – again.

Let's Google the answer when we get back folks. The loser buys us all a drink. How's that?

So decisive.

Miriam glares but Gordon doesn't really like confrontation so moves to the next question to bring peace.

What is the capital of Lithuania?

Oh dear!

Chester is lovely.

The sun is out, and the guide makes us laugh

You're from the Wirral he says.

I've heard of that.

He tells us about the clock put up for the 1857 Jubilee.

The clock maker had so many orders he couldn't deliver in time and the clock face was cardboard for two years till the real one came. Fancy that!

The historical Albion pub was interesting.

And I think that's where we lost Gilda in her chiffon.

Back to the bus, back to the Wirral, all well fed and happy.

The bus now doing the travelling instead of weary feet.

I can smell a good mood - then Beryl's seat collapsed.

She will fiddle, and the morning's palaver began all over again.

Who would sit where and with whom.

Uproar!

At that point Miriam grabs the clipboard from me

You're not firm enough with this lot.

– Oh dear!

This lot - A very unfortunate phrase. Everyone bristled

and tension rose.

I'm not pleased either as Miriam keeps the clipboard,

my symbol of power,

Effectively deposing me.

The driver dilutes the stress by releasing the throttle.

I HAVE TO REMIND MYSELF

At heart, we're all good friends.

I was right about the Albion pub.

Gilda is an extrovert, to put her flamboyance, politely.

She has had a liquid lunch and is impolitely drunk.

She's always had a thing about Joe since his wife died,

The whole village knows.

Now she flings caution to the winds, displaces his sister

Betty and is all over Joe.

If we're all to remain friends Gilda should be disciplined.

But what to do?

I make a mental note to exclude her from the next trip to

Oxford.

Then I realise Miriam has still got my clipboard.

I'm really annoyed now and vow to abdicate.

She can organise the next outing.

After all they're her friends as well as mine.

I continue the remainder of the journey next to the angel, Gabriel.

He's wearing a tweed suit in warm brown, the colour of his eyes.

It's a sober cloth and dependable like himself.

And quietly we arrange to go somewhere on our own next time.

We're the **best** of friends.

7

THE MATING GAME

Sylvia was my friend because nobody else would tolerate her. They found her weird, I found her alternately intriguing and annoying.

She dressed in the latest from the local charity shops. She had money but, one of her theories kicked in, 'you don't find "vintage" anywhere in the mall shops. Everything is neutered to comply with diktats from the fashion houses. Give me a bygone 50's dirndl or a hobble skirt any day'.

She would come out with all kinds of ideas some of them believable, such as, before the end of the 21st century we would be communicating with alien races across the universe. Not a mind busting possibility but most people thought she was just grandstanding for attention. In her defence she always backed up her statements with some obscure reference source. I took the trouble to check out some of them. A number came from esoteric books or online. Unfortunately, some were from people, like Sylvia, who had had flights of fancy on falling asleep: developed on waking, at which point the dream should have been forgotten. Nevertheless, I stuck with Sylvia until she moved away from our Town.

I missed her. I was wedged between neighbours and friends whose conversation revolved around the Royal family and speculations on divorce among celebrities. I enjoy gossip, like the next, but a menu of starters that don't lead on to anything more satisfying, dulls the appetite for more.

I was reminded of Sylvia when I met up with Sam: a seriously possible partner for life. At that point memories of Sylvia and her potty ideas kicked in. Sylvia theorized that we were all animals. Animals have an acute sense of smell: very underused and underestimated in the human animal. The animal kingdom uses this sense to sniff out sexual partners. It was possibly more reliable, she argued, for us to find lasting partners this way. After all, 'Smell is something they can't fake.' She dismissed good looks as going the way of Dorian Gray over time. 'No guide at all.' Words were also ignored as a lead to character. 'There are always sweet ones to turn our head. They turn sour after the wedding.' There was always lots to argue about. We then had a good laugh about exploring the smell theory and how to checkout a partner's 'bits'.

Before the arrival of Sam, the possible love of my life, I had been through Frank, Nevil, Boris and Joseph. It was an interesting bouquet of blokes. I met Frank in a railway carriage going down to London. He was dressed in the uniform of academics: cord trousers, bobbled sweater and a jacket with sagging pockets. Not my type at all. I liked "Smart". But he was interesting. He believed in the Planet and knew a lot about bats and bees. We ended up walking London parks and sat watching the mute swans in Regent's Park. There we ate sandwiches instead of a proper lunch. Looking back, they were egg and not very fresh. Frank spoke as he chomped away and, unfair or not, egg became associated with Frank and his saggy pockets. Despite an unbridled fling in varied parts of wild nature, Frank 'good egg' became Frank 'bad egg'.

Nevil followed in a tailored suit and expensive after shave. Everything about Nevil was straight lines: Creased trousers and belief in equally controlled neat ideas. There was never a whiff of egg around Nevil. Nevil was unreal, a bit like a show home which has just been hoovered and polished. His odour was neutral.

Boris was all blubber but had charm. 'Charm' in my dictionary means, 'he listens to me'. That is a very seductive approach. But, in the end Boris' blubber let him down. The smell of the sea and the landed whale threw all thoughts of romance overboard.

That left the path clear for Joseph. I cannot now think why I let him into my life: a history buff who looked as if he needed dusting off and that was his undoing. His dust particles got up my nose and I sneezed my way through two weeks of courtship.

Then along came Sam.

We met on a jogging path early morning. Sam smelled of the morning sunshine, newly mown grass and a sprinkle of spring rain. Even his sweaty gear just belonged in the mix shaken and stirred with the exhilaration of the exercise. It defined Sam, very unfairly perhaps, but I had to smell Sam, like an addiction to morning coffee, before I could start my day.

I'm hunting down Sylvia's address as I ponder, to point out the success attached to her theory of smell and to scribe the invitation to my wedding with Sam.

Barbara Maitra

8

TIME FOR NATURE

We enter this world governed by the rules of nature.

The nurse is counting, *contractions every seventy seconds, now every thirty seconds*. They become more intense and regular, and the nurse gets to work. She looks at the clock on the wall. It's 10.30 am. This is followed by *you have a lovely, healthy baby boy, Mrs Jones.*

Recording the time of birth doesn't really matter unless you are going to produce a horoscope for the baby. The healthy baby is not inclined to notice the clock on the wall either. Nature, not the clock is in charge: he wakes when he's hungry, cries when he's wet, yells when his stomach pains. Nature is still in command. It won't be long before he learns that nature and the clock on the wall share commands: eat your cornflakes, you're starting nursery today and the doors open at nine thirty. Who's a lucky boy?

Then, put *your shoes on. It's 8.30, you'll be late for school.*

And further down the line, *where were you at 2.15? You missed your lecture on Viking Law.*

And today, he's peeling a parking notice off his windscreen, *Parking charge exceeded by ten minutes. To be paid before 10am on the 10th of this month.*

It has taken twenty-three years to reduce the wilful baby to a man who scuttles like a spider across a carpet, to the council offices, to pay his fine, before the clock strikes 10am on Monday.

Let's call him Ben. He is a brown boy with bracken coloured hair and eyes the colour of chestnuts. He is young, lithe and jobless. He sits on a bench in the park but there is nothing of the vagrant about him. He is still suited and booted, reflecting on the job he has just lost. It was called a job, but he was warned it was a stopgap and pension-less. Now he is having a few moments and wonders where his life is going.

He looks at his watch. It tells him it is lunchtime.

He takes an apple out of his pocket and looks up at the sky for inspiration. This is 'thinking time' as unfocused as the birds rising and falling in the thermals of air. He has no positive ideas about his future. He stays so long on the bench that time just rolls on with its repetitive tick, ticks, into a nadir of inactivity. But this is not wasted time. Thoughts that are scattered like paper in the wind simply circulate his options. All he needs to do is grab. Stimulated, inspired, emboldened, Ben holds on to one of those papers and decides.

Ten years on, Ben is in blessed time that comes from a loving relationship with wife Margaret and two children. He is still a brown man, still lithe from the tennis he plays. He is settled in a home where everyone is governed by the clock: the wife who works 9 to 5, as a teacher. The children are now grown up sufficiently to have sleepovers but regulated by *home tomorrow in time for dinner*. And Ben himself is doing time. Not behind bars but the other side of a glass panel where time moves on to the turn of a page concerning the breakdown of a marriage or defaulting on a contract.

It is noon and a winter sun makes a jaundiced yellow puddle on Ben's desk. Ben's stomach is grumbling which makes him consult his watch. It shows fifteen minutes past his usual lunchtime. He then has the first of a few errant thoughts: *I'm hungry, why should I have to consult my watch?* His thoughts now take a more rebellious direction: questioning, *what happened to make us a slave to the clock?*

He knows the answer to this. Looking down at the files on his desk he appreciates that that is where the money comes from to give him the comfortable life he enjoys. He flicks the pages exposing his timetable - in court at 11am tomorrow with Morgan Lily versus The Council, 12am the day after. The clock calendar rolls on to the month end with the case for Sully v Crown. It is a satisfying case load. But the worm of discomfort which has lodged in his brain after the day he questioned 'living by the clock,' has not gone away.

It remains with him six months later when he and

Margaret go on a tour to South Africa.

Ben, the stolid family man, disappears.

There are questions asked about how, why and when: theories postulated about abduction, sudden illness, and accidents. Someone saw a shadow in the scrub, someone saw a horse, someone heard a noise he couldn't describe but no-one took any notice. There are police searches, but a man who does not want to be found has an advantage.

Ben is working as a hired hand on an isolated cattle farm, numerous in the vastness that is Africa. The idea of escape came during the bus tour he and Margaret took showing life in the bush outside the city. He daringly mounted the roving horse. He felt as if it was Bucephalus – and he was flying to freedom.

His only human contact is the boss, eccentric owner, and his dog. From two bruising encounters Ben has already diagnosed the scruffy animal as a trained killer. He now keeps his distance. Ben has adapted to sleeping out in the field in a little hut he put together with tools from the eccentric. He rises with the sun to drive the cattle to the water holes; he fixes the fences against baboon interference and then thinks about life. He thinks about past times when life was governed by the rising sun and phases of the moon. How both controlled daily lives: the animals we herded and the crops we grew. He decides he is happy recreating that life. He is still a brown man but one who has lost his suit and grown a beard.

Two years into this escape, Ben is re-thinking his choice. He is very busy, still connected with the cattle. Tomorrow he is helping with their inoculation. Another sporadic employee, a black man called Joseph will provide more muscle to hold the barriers as the cattle pass Ben's needle, one by one. He feels worthy. But as he sits watching the sun go down other thoughts come with the dark. There is no-one there when he makes improvements to his log hut. No-one there to say 'well done' as he makes the roof impermeable. He admits to needing that lift. The boys would have said 'well done

Dad', words to remember with a warm feeling of being admired.

Tending the cattle helps him pay his way and he collects that from the eccentric down the dirt road. The scruffy killer animal slavers as he approaches the owner. The eccentric is here to be alone, needing no-one. He barely glances at Ben as he hands out a wage. Ben jiggles the coinage, enough to buy a beer. But a glass has to be shared with someone for it to have meaning. Ben is missing a 'someone'.

He is still in awe of the beauty of nature. He revels in the colours of the sunset as it sinks behind the purple hills. There is a growing desire to share that experience also with someone., someone like Margaret. Margaret, the last sight of her surrounded by a noisy crowd, gesticulating, the driver hustling everyone to get back in the bus and Margaret in tears. The picture triggers the chemical that produces tears and his eyes fill.

The cattle brush against each other and lick in an

act of grooming. They huddle together as a herd when heavy rains come, they are all huddled protectively under the tree, mid field. Ben makes the final admission that man is an animal also and needs to belong.

A year later Ben is back, enclosed in his family. There was a passport to re-entry: much discussion about crises in life and what Ben did. Much soul searching followed by many promises. On the night of their peace treaty, as they name it, Margaret buys him a new watch to replace the one he had thrown in the cattle pond. She observes him closely. *Will this make him feel handcuffed to time once more?*

Without hesitation he winds it round his wrist and admires the black face, declaring it, 'stylish'. Duplicitously she opens a bottle of wine and plays a song from her re-found love of the group TAKE THAT. Much of it in a minor key gives the words a poignancy:

This is the life we've been given,
so, open your mind and start living.

72

9

HESITATION

She stepped aside from the stream of water and reached for the towel. She took a step back and nearly stood on the thing making its way menacingly in her direction. Dread sent her, shuddering, to the corner of the bathroom. There she glared at it, and it sat motionless as if weighing up where to attack.

She was not going to move from the safety of the corner, so she had time to stand and regret booking an Air B'n'B without checking it out properly. An up-market hotel would not have produced the monster that was studying her. She eyed a twig-like broom in the corner opposite. But everyone knows, cockroaches would be the last living things to survive a nuclear attack so why would the broom be anything other than a wet room sweeper? It was certainly not a weapon. The insect moved its feelers. She could almost hear its evil thoughts, 'You are in my sights now'.

She was well aware of phobias and how people dealt with them. She had watched TV masochists hold spiders in their hands and stroke snakes. 'Stroke', that was a good word, she would **have** a stroke if she was asked to do anything but run.

Naked and despite the sunshine she was feeling shivery. That demanded some kind of action. Should she chance reaching for the broom to fend off the menace till she reached the door and safety?

It turned its body like a shining missile and fixed a path to her feet.

She climbed up on the toilet seat surveying the next hurdle. How to get the cover down whilst standing on the basin rim. Holding the cistern, she managed a tricky one-foot, next foot manoeuvre and the lid fell with a bang.

Now I know where you are. Her head followed the feelers up then down and sideways as if being conducted. The rhythm spelled NE.. ME..SIS. Time to ponder a further move but terrorised decision making is poor stuff. Just time to recall that She had lived in a hot country where lizards on the wall was the décor together with cockroaches. Their local name was *ARSHOLA.*

'How appropriate.'

Nevertheless, with total recall she had seen people nonchalantly pick them up between their toes and flick them outside. No roadkill there. And, she also didn't want to kill. She had used brushes before and battered them. It was worse seeing them lose their innards and still not die. James Bond and the poisonous spider episode from Dr NO entered her head. It had crawled up his naked torso plodding slowly, pausing for sips of sweat along the way. The thoughts of a fellow sufferer steadied her a little.

But the stand-off on the toilet seat was precarious and brought her no closer to giving her a decision. She speculated once more about the broom. Even if she got there and touched the thing, could she bear the shock which would ride up the twigs like electricity.

And then, a bang on the door. A B'n'B shared

bathroom after all. This time it was welcomed as a plus, a deus ex machine device. The cockroach scuttled towards the drain outlet away from the vibrating door. She descended from the toilet and sped across the slippery floor. A fall was better than an encounter with the evil poised at the drain grid.

Hanging on the doorknob was the cranky old man from room 15. Her naked body, flying past, did not register in the face of his own obsession,

'Why do you always leave the floor swimming in water?

10

LIVING THE FAIRYTALE

Like Hans Anderson's Red Shoes, the jacket wore **her** with magical influence. Laura spotted it from the charity shop alcove which was her street B&B – well B, there was rarely breakfast involved.

It was opulent enough to have royal connections. When she looked in the mirror, she felt compelled to reinvent herself. Maybe it had belonged to the *Wicked Queen.*

Laura wore it to Alfie's party where buyers, with acres of real estate, and oozing gold requiring tourniquets, were present. Alfie's pictures dressed the walls: she, the centre of the room. Everyone wanted a piece of Alfie, recently of the streets. It only takes one sale to the right person just as one match can set the world alight. He had become the opera of the art world.

The jacket blazed above black clad legs providing a pedestal for its spectacle. She stood holding a Margherita. Women grudgingly appraised her skinny figure wondering how it suddenly defined sex.

An Eastern prince was expected. Failing to buy a local football club he arrived, pockets bulging with money and noticed her. He had sniffed something which had him swinging from the chandeliers. Climbing down, he slowly threaded his way through the horde to the apparition centre stage and offered her a full glass.

'How did you know I was drinking Margheritas?'

'I'm not very clever, just spotted the salt round the rim'.

You might not be clever, but you are very rich.

'Thankyou', she said demurely.

'You a personal friend of Alfie's?'

'Indeed. Next door neighbours.' A fair description. Before fame elevated him Alfie occupied the bakery B&B alcove, next to hers. 'I'm always invited to grace his exhibitions'.

'It's hungry work spending money. Would you

care to grace my table at the Ritz?'

That was the first outing for the jacket. After the second and third she had no more worries about food or accommodation.

Like the charity jacket, she called the process, redistribution of wealth.

Barbara Maitra

11

SENSORY RECALL

Ears were glued to the radio before the 50's. Then TV spread like a measles epidemic. Our greatest entertainment before those inventions was life and death on the streets where everyone knew everyone or was related. Kingdoms of their own. And the death of a granny: anybody's granny, on any street drew the crowds. I was reminded of this when, as a journalist, I returned to photograph the Back-to-backs in a place called Brightside, Sheffield. The council which gave this name to the area had a massive sense of humour: either that or the dust, circulating from the blast furnaces, blinded them.

My observations, as a ten-year-old came back to me. Not to be dismissed: at that age kids are sharp, and memories etch into a brain forever. At ten, one is not invisible but ignored at the eavesdropping level of table talk: so, recall of direct speech can be trusted also. Most of all pictures. The dying street granny lay on the iron bedstead. Her skeleton had made no impression on the sheets covering her. We should have been able to trace a body, alive or dead by an outline. There were no shoulders, no little mound of a belly, no thighs linking the architecture which terminates in the feet. Nothing to show how she had washed, cleaned and raised children, muscles and humour intact.

Her head rested on a pillow covered in ticking. That pillow set the parameters of cliff-edge poverty which had been her life. No white, Oxford-cornered pillowcases here, no co-ordinated colour scheme: that was a shade called threadbare. The skin on her face dripped like candle wax to the edge of the covers. She had kept most of her teeth, but her mouth now emitted only snorts. Not long to go now.

Drawn like buzzards to carrion the event was observed by the neighbours who dropped in from time to time watching that all was as it should be. Alice, the unmarried daughter, was now having her moment of glory as she maintained her bedside vigil. The 'droppers in' supplied her with endless tea and arrowroot biscuits. The first and last time in her life she would be waited on. She felt grand and deserving. Looking after the bones under the sheet had been her whole life. Duty. Slowly her own self had diminished to a formless bundle within her loose knitted cardigan. This had a sourness woven into every plain and purl stitch: a picture and smell of neglect.

Remnants of family drifted in, and then, out, for a smoke. No-one wanted to be accused of delivering the final blow to an ailing granny. Peer pressure put them on alert to maintain appearances. Then there were other family units who made themselves scarce to continue ongoing feuds outside: all gestures out of respect for granny but where grudges nursed over the years spurted a new life.

The kitchen range, newly black-leaded was approved: Alice was not letting things slip. Under the mantelshelf was a wire festooned with tea towels and a pair of directoire knickers picking up the scent of a stew pot hanging over the coal fire. This granny had no will, nothing to leave so remnants of life had to be held on to.

Alice feeds her a spoonful of water. Granny's hands appear from under the sheets, and she appears to grab food which she steers to her mouth. Those policing the event strain forward. *Is she coming round?*

The talk outside centres on Alice. *Might she look for a future for herself when the end comes? All agree duty has been done so far and maybe she has left it too late. Look at her.*

Street granny's last effort, reaching for something took a lot of energy, too much, Granny fades with a whisper that hardly stirs the sheet.

This is a community, its own fiefdom which policed itself. It had no care for the doctor's verdict. When Alice appeared in a new outfit complete with high heels, Brightside delivered its own judgement. That granny had taken a long time to go and then, suddenly......

No doubt daughter Alice took that manky pillow and smothered her. She always was impatient.

Such was the soap opera of the day.

Barbara Maitra

12

INCONSEQUENTIAL POSTCARDS

I discovered My Aunt Lilian in the attic.

That was on one of my frequent visits to check on my mother, then 70. We had the usual exchanges as I dropped the holdall and stumbled into her sitting room.

'Mum, if you'd come to live with me in London, I'd not have this back-and-forth odyssey. How are you anyway?' I gave her a hug and kissed her cheek. She always smelled of Lily of the Valley. The hug confirmed more than any words that she was still steady on her feet and eating well.

'I'm OK and likely to stay that way if I remain with the fresh air up here. I bet if you blow your nose now the tissue will be black. What's up your nose is on your lungs.' It was the usual rebuttal of my invitation to come and live near me, then, 'Here, I've made your favourites.' She placed a dish in front of me and turned aside. It ended the argument and I sat down to a plate of her scones, cream, jam – the lot.

'You're right about the air down there but, that's where the action is.'

'Hmm' was the only comment, followed by, 'how long are you here for? I'd like you to go up the attic and get the briefcase down with the important stuff in it'.

'No problem.' Fluffy, the pseudo-Persian cat sidled up to me. 'I hope it's not a 'Will' thing. Re-directing my inheritance to the cat's home?'

Mum laughed at that. I didn't need reassurance, but I was curious.

As I went upstairs –

'Mr Bob has done your room out. White spot on a baby blue ground. I hope your nightie isn't the same pattern or you'll be invisible.'

'Nice thought' I yelled back. 'Attic first.'

The stairs were not steep but uncarpeted and a bit dusty. Mum hadn't been up here for some time I guessed. At the top, it was hard to look anywhere and remain unemotional. My doll's house sat next to ice skates that had ruined my career as an Olympic sprinter. Unconsciously I reached down and scratched the scar. I leaned over tarnished trophies searching for the briefcase. I hoped she would remember the code to unlock it otherwise we'd spend the weekend on testing to destruction. Behind it was a box with embroidered cloths and some postcards.

As a magazine editor I fall hard for pictures, so my hand went out to the pack. Elastic bands held them together. One withered piece of elastic fell away twisting like a worm.

'Are you OK up there, Sally?'

'Sure. Coming down now,' And down I went, both hands full.

'Oh good. It's a bit battered, isn't it?' Then her eyes widened as they fixed on the postcards.

'What on earth?'

'Pretty, aren't they?' I said flashing the top picture.' **You** must think so. They were stowed away like treasure, probably since Adam was a lad.

I removed the second elastic band. 'San Francisco: who do we know lives there?' Mum's interest was no longer with the briefcase, she was staring at the cards. I turned San Francisco over. No message. *What was the point, I wondered.* The next card was Alcatraz. A lonely, menacing lump sitting in tranquil waters. I turned that one over and read, 'Wish you were here.' I laughed and passed it to Mum. 'Somebody loves you.'

'That's Lilian,' she said. 'Typical of my sister.'

'Your sister? I have an aunt. Why don't I know about this?'

'I'd forgotten about those cards. That's digging up the past.'

'You forgot a sister. How could you?'

'Calm down Sally, I had no option. Can you see any addresses on the cards? No. **She** cut **us** off'.

'But you kept the cards.'

'If your father was alive, he would have thrown them out. Yes, I kept them. She married his best friend then divorced him and just flitted, leaving him broken hearted. You think men don't feel these things, but they do. It's not just the humiliation of "being disposed of". She made no secret of using the money from the divorce to go and look for a more exciting partner.'

'Oh dear. Tut-tut Auntie Lilian. So then what?'

'Lilian was beautiful. Younger than me by two years. She was so pretty. When we went to fancy dress parties, she was the fairy, I was a gypsy with a tea towel round my head.'

'So, pretty or not she didn't land a husband in the USA?'

'Not that we know. Probably no-one rich enough. She made no secret of looking for money as well as a husband. Turn the next card up. These have never been discussed since I hid them away.'

That card was from Italy and a picture of the Vatican. I turned over the card. '*No point in looking for a husband here. Off to Budapest.*'

Lilian was amusing to a point, and I surrendered

to the flamboyance of her journey.

There followed pictures of Buda castle staring over the Danube at Pest. Overleaf was scrawled, *A bit hairy but I have a little Hungarian. I'll get by.* Did she actually speak Hungarian or was this another message with a double meaning? The next card showed pictures of the Danube. Overleaf was written *Dropped the little Hungarian. He was too hairy.* So that was it, not a smattering of the language. I wondered where she went next: she was halfway through Europe and running out of husband territory.

A few Danube pictures came, all blank on the reverse until one of Melk castle in Austria. I Knew it, I'd been there. A handsome creation hanging over the Danube, admiring itself in the waters. Overleaf was the message, *decisions have been made. I've settled on an Austrian. This might be my home next week. Schloss Lilian.* Then silence.

'No more cards came Mum said. I guess if she married an Austrian, it would be about the time Hitler took over. Late 1930s. And she vanished from our lives'. Mum's eyes filled up.

'It's hard to vanish completely nowadays Mum'. I could see that she was still upset. 'I've told you, it's hard to disappear in this day and age. I'll find her if that's what you want. I have an army of foot soldiers down in London. We'll find her. And when I do, you can play the big sister and give her a good blasting'.

*****

There was a bit of hyperbole employed in describing my two assistants down in London as 'an army of foot soldiers'. But, once they had finished painting their nails and shared their nightly adventures, I would not have exchanged them for two bloodhounds when it came to tracking. German records of everything they have done and achieved are legend in their detail. Val and Dodi brought back Lilian's story within a month. The cold facts they unearthed told a heartwarming story.

It seems that on arrival in Vienna Lilian ceased

making her own crazy plans and fulfilled the Hindu philosophy of unrolling the carpet on which the pattern of her fate was scribed. She met Dieter Schultz, a policeman. His name labelled him a law enforcer by tradition. Their names, like ours have a history. A Fletcher here made arrows in middle England; a Pinder was responsible for impounding loose cattle. The Austrian Schultz's were headmen in medieval times and enforced the law and the 20th century Dieter Schultz was no exception. It seems that Lilian was also, by romantic tradition, transformed by her love affair.

She had exchanged her Schloss vision for an apartment, like most Austrian citizens. Val and Dodi found her living on the ground floor in Wipplingerstrasse, near the Jewish quarter. They brought back pictures of a 68-year-old Lilian, her prettiness now matured into a finely sculpted face. She was living alone, beloved Dieter long gone. He had supported the movement for a democratic Germany which grew out of the Weimar Republic. Those ideas were swamped by the Nazi machinery of Hitler, and Dieter, as a dissident, like many others, disappeared. Lilian herself was taken away but refused to discuss with my assistants what happened to her. As Val and Dodi left, Lilian used the two sticks lying by her chair, to propel herself to the door and they saw her twisted legs for the first time.

They left carrying a postcard, for me and a reference to my mother. She had written her address and a message, 'Apologies to big sister and I have now stopped looking for a husband. I'm still in love with the last one.'

We did follow up visits of course hoping to re-unite Mum with sister Lilian, but Lilian died following the last operation to straighten her mangled legs. The sisters never managed to meet up.

Mum had the last word as an epitaph for Lilian. 'It was some sort of closure for me knowing that after all that wandering, she found happiness. Of course, I forgive her. And I had never forgotten her. My pretty, flaky, selfish sister grew up at last. Thank you, Dieter Schultz.'

13

THINGS LOOK DIFFERENT

The full moon slid from behind the one cloud in the sky.

The man in the shirt was busy shovelling leaves with his massive hands. Silver reflected from the sweat glistening on powerful arms. How quickly the leaves put the light out covering the twisted body of the girl. The halo of blood however continued to reflect diamond specks like a tiara. Normally moonshine is benign, its softness breeds romance. Tonight, it was merciless picking out the scene below.

One last look and a sudden mind change ended his activity. He picked up his backpack and started to run. It was a long way to safety.

The moon followed his journey through the woods. The leaves flickered the steady light as he pounded through the trees. It turned him into a satyr: no longer a man in mountain boots and commercial shirt. He leaped over fallen logs and wove through low branches.

The moonlight picked out the tarmac ahead. The dead blacktop looked grim: unyielding. By contrast the man's tension relaxed. Lithely he leaped into his car and sped away.

Moonlight is fading now. Wisps of mist curl up around the abandoned body in the wood like angelic ghosts keeping watch.

An hour later an approaching police siren announces a rising sun. Growling its way through the rutted forest paths it halts beside the body. Three men unload together with the man who bolted.

'Let's get these leaves away. Did you not have a coat or anything else to cover her?'

'Nothing. We parked up and walked. She fell down the cut there. It fills up with water so, gently as I could I pulled her up to safety.'

She stirred as the sun burnished the metal on life saving gear. The blue world turned lemon yellow, and she smiled.

14

ME TO YOU TO ME

TUESDAY

Darling Rob - I'm sitting at the computer writing this email. You can picture that can't you? When you write back tell me where you are and what you are doing so, I can have a picture of you, in the moment. Pics would be good.

Six months is a long time. I didn't realise when I agreed to your working away that it would be this hard. Of course, there wasn't much choice, it's your job to troubleshoot. Just a pity the trouble is in Sri Lanka.

It's funny, but to emphasise how I miss you I'm noticing all the things that are not there. It's ironic really.

There's no more noise from your chair facing the telly. I always thought cricket was a quiet, slow game but you made it a pretty major event. Every wicket that fell I thought we'd lost the chair. I bet you miss that. It's good for your back and we took a long time choosing it. And saving up for it! The things we did without to buy that chair. Do you remember? The people in the shops must have thought we were daft trying every chair, this way and that way. I wonder how your back is coping without it. Tell me.

I've now got the bathroom to myself, but I miss harassing you in the morning. Knocking on the door and asking if you were reading War and Peace in there? Have you ever read War & Peace? I haven't but it's a saying, isn't it? You always said the same thing when you eventually came out, 'Can't you digest your breakfast without yelling at me woman?

'Woman'!

Do you know what I miss the most, and don't laugh? Every time we went anywhere special you asked me, 'Does this tie go?' I can hear you laughing now. Don't deny it. I know you. I'm not kidding. Tie moments were OUR moments. Like seeing you across a room full of people. They all melted away when our eyes met. Only you and I were in that room.

I think I might be feeling a bit sorry for myself, so I'll finish off today on a good note. Our Tabby, Mr Tibbs, misses you more than I do if possible. She scowls at me when I put biscuits in her bowl. So it's not true that cats are full of cupboard love only. I feed her and all I get is looks. Do the tigers where you are look anything like him? maybe you've not seen any so far.

Take care. I love you.

Betsy.

FRIDAY

Darling Rob. That was a lovely photo you sent. Tell that scientist cum model not to stand so close next time. You look well and I'm pleased you know what the problem is with the tea bushes. Maybe the quick diagnosis will bring you home sooner. *Birds Eye Spot* doesn't sound like an infection more like something picked out because it's so pretty. It seems to me that a bad fungus should have a name to match. *Funglebladderwhiff maybe.* I guess the company will be pleased you've nailed the problem.

Every time I drink a cup of tea, I think of you, when I'm not otherwise thinking of you. That's not very often.

Gossip – Jane (anything but plain now) popped in to see me. She was in hospital having varicose veins looked at, so we heard. She was out of circulation for so long, we all wondered. Well, now we know, she's had more than veins looked at. I'm positive her nose is straighter, her cheeks fuller and her backside artistically reduced. She looks a million. It hasn't helped her keep hubby at home though. This time he's gone for good. She wasn't very kind about your being away. *Absence makes the heart grow fonder* I said. She came back at me, quite vicious, *Absence makes the spouse to wander*. By the time she left I was looking at your photo and seeing only the model scientist blocking out part of your new bush shirt. I'm talking rubbish 'cos she's left me a bit down hearted. I'm taking your photo to bed with me. You will be the last thing I see before I close my eyes and sleep.

Take care. I love you, Betsy.

A WEEK LATER

Darling Rob – Nice set of photos. You look so well. Despite your *Gingeriness* you have managed a tan. The countryside does look beautiful, and I like your suggestion that it could be a holiday place for us next year.

And yes, I'm jealous. Deal with it.

It's weird you were talking holidays. I had all our albums out last night and watched a whole lot of that walking tour in Portugal. Then I looked back at the following year when we did *pots.* I fell in love with you all over again on that holiday. It was my idea. I'm the artistic one and talked you into it. Your hands were not made for throwing clay but you were game and loved me enough to go along. You didn't whinge every time your efforts collapsed. And there were many. Don't deny it. I have pictures of some of the more spectacular ones. You were so sweet. You just turned round and kissed me looking at my effort. *That bowl will sell for at least a million. Well done. As soon as we get back, we'll go into business together. I'll market your talent. Then we'll retire to Portugal and make love all day.*

Here's a puzzle for you. What did I reply? Answers on a post card or your next email will do.

I've had a lot of interest in the wall plaques I did in the summer. Sold two at £40 each.

I'm going to buy me some of that glamour Jane got for herself. Maybe not cost as much – just something out of a bottle from Boots to celebrate your homecoming.

Take more care. That scratch on your knee looked a bit fierce. I hope you have medics on site. And you never mentioned your back. How is it?

Goodnight – Betsy loves you, as you know.

FOLLOWING WEEK

Darling Rob – I see you have found a remedy for your back pain. I'm pleased but insanely jealous of the scientist who arranged your special masseur. I'm guessing – no, hoping it wasn't her.

I'm sounding naggy n' wifey and all the things I vowed I would never be. I'm feeling a bit insecure and blowing my top to you because you're the only one who cares. If

I talk to my sister, she'll listen for a minute then her eyes will glaze over and she'll trot out something to shut me up, 'don't be stupid. *Rob is Rob. You were meant for each other. He's the last person in the world to play away. Do you like my new dress?'* You care and I care. Who else will listen earnestly and care about that tiny pimple I had on my bum. I'm telling myself that's what lovers do, and I'm convinced. This is the last jealous bit you'll hear from me. I'm really pleased about your back but hanging on to your chair still.

Cats don't talk but they have body language. Mr Tibbs is telling me he loves you, not me. I've told him I don't care. You love me more than him.

I found some more missing things that remind me you're not here. Your filing system on the floor has gone. The place is so damned tidy, and empty. The grass has grown back on the lawn where you practised your putting. No more baldy patch. Even if I have to use the scissors, I'll put the track back before you come home. I collected your posh Italian shoes from the menders who repaired that bit that came apart. They smell like you, in the nicest possible way. I suppose it would be too weird to take them to bed with me. You never actually told me how much you were cheated in Rome. But, like you, I just love the shoes. They are the 'dress up' you, not the green welly botanist you.

Yes, you got the answer right. The answer was 'I'll stop all the clocks.'

I'm attaching a photo of the makeover me. Do you like that colour lipstick?

Loads of love

Betsy

AFTER 6 MONTHS

You're coming home Thursday. Wonderful.

Just so you know, Mr Tibbs got tired of waiting and has gone to live next door. That's what cats do.

But I'm here. At last, I can tell you that I love you to your face. It doesn't go down too well on paper does it?

Yours always

Betsy

15

A WARTIME CHRISTMAS

Alice Murray has just made a bread pudding. That's what war does to you at Christmas time: take the substitutes that rationing gives you, combine them with skill and pretend it's Christmas pudding. Well, those skills in this particular pudding were brought from Dublin where her family had to make do and mend whether there was a war on or not. Butter, dried fruit, tangy peel, whisky, sugar, eggs: all the things that went into a celebration cake and puddings are rationed or hard to get.

She should not grumble about Christmas puddings when Lottie next door had celebrated her wedding with a look-alike cardboard cake. It looked good but heavens knew what was under it when the cardboard was lifted. There were some terrible compromises in war. She was pleased to forfeit the powdered egg to her pudding, better there than have it repeat on you the whole day after a scrambled egg breakfast. As Alice lifts the steaming cloth out of the pan, the smell from a few raisins and a spot of rum pleases her; she had done better than Lottie's mother with the wedding non-cake. The pudding is an act of creation.

She straightens her pinny, it has small flower prints scattered randomly and each day it is changed for a similar one, clean and starched. That reminds her, she must iron one for tomorrow, Christmas Eve. A hairpin falls out of the net restraining her hair.

Thank goodness that didn't go into the tripe and onions.

She picks it up and reinserts it into hair that still has shades of auburn despite her being sixty and having had nine children. Three of those children were lost before the war started. She can guarantee that you never get over losing a child but now, grieving has been replaced with worry for the four sons serving in the forces. Cooking allows her mind to wander because tripe and onions requires little skill after forty years' practice.

She thinks of Billy. Always the rebellious one. He's going to be in the glasshouse for Christmas. She puzzles over the name and decides it must be army slang for a detention centre, but the reasoning behind the name eludes her. Of course, breaking out of barracks to visit that wife of his deserved detention. She does not like Judy, no religion and 'fast'. What can you expect coming from the east end of the town?

Son Bob will be alright. He's army, on the ground, looking after engines. But Dan is up in the air, in planes, flying every night and now the sound of an aircraft makes her tremble. She has no idea where son Peter is: In the jungle somewhere.

At this stage she is driven to the parlour to say a prayer to Saint Theresa. She downs tools and hurries, lifting her heavy leg over the step so hastily it makes her wince. But this might be just the moment a prayer is needed: a jungle snake might be ready to strike Peter and even now the searchlights might be picking out Dan's aircraft over Germany.

Saint Theresa is in a glass dome, smiling, pristine and dustless. The saint, known as the Little Flower, is Alice's favourite. The parlour still smells a bit musty even though she has opened it up for the last two days. They all make fun of her, locking the door, but she reminds them it is opened on feast days and holidays only, used sparingly, to keep it looking good, year after year. Every stick of furniture in that room has been paid for and it has to last, as does everything in her house. Under her stewardship, the kitchen pine table is scrubbed, the lino in the kitchen swept, the peg rugs shaken and the front step donkey-stoned every day.

After her word with Saint Theresa, she turns and takes a look round her parlour. It has a lot of green that reminds her of Ireland. The antimacassars on the armchairs are deep green like the fields at home and the cushions on the sofa are a softer green velvet. She is proud of her home, but not too proud; That is a sin which she would not like to reveal to Father Kerry in confession. She closes the door behind her and hangs the key on the hook by the door.

Pa is at the bottom of the garden looking after his rhubarb. He says he is doing his bit, digging for Victory but why is it only rhubarb he grows? Ha! She knows the answer, it's for his bowels no matter what else he might say.

She calls him into dinner. He likes tripe and onions and tonight she has kept back a bit of ham for supper. That makes her trek to the cellar head to see the bread position. Bread, bread and potatoes, so important and here they are, years into the war and handing over BU's for bread. Bread Units! And they are counted; you can't get an extra slice out of them. What a terrible thing war is for a housewife. They have a small chicken for Christmas and the leftovers will make rissoles with potatoes for Boxing Day. She is suddenly sorry about the rhubarb thoughts. She has to admit that Pa does do his bit with the potatoes.

He comes in with his muddy boots, so he gets a

shout reminding him that she's just swept up. Out comes his pipe, (she knew that would be next) and he fills the bowl with tobacco. It's a nuisance but Alice likes the smell, it normalises the day. It's a routine that the war has not smashed: the milkman, the postman, the six o'clock news, they all go on. She loves her religion for the same reason. It goes on with its comforting liturgy giving backbone to her day. She has a sneaking suspicion that Pa does not really believe but they do not discuss that and if he stays abed of a Sunday, she accepts that, after a lifetime of work, his back is killing him. It makes life easier. Presently Pa knocks the ash out of the pipe before he sits to dinner. Alice is really aggravated now. She reminds him that she has black leaded the range and he has messed it up with the trail of powder from his pipe, streaking the grate.

Mid tripe and onions he asks her what they are having for Christmas and she tells him one of the few jokes she knows, answering, 'a run round the table and a kick at the cat.'

Out of habit he ignores that and continues with his dinner.

'I don't suppose our Billy will get even that,' he reminds her.

That upsets Alice and she would like to say that all that bad blood in Billy came from his side of the family. Pa has a hard streak which she sees in Billy. Alice has never really forgiven Pa for taking her away from Ireland and the cruel words he used as the boat sailed away from the harbour. 'Take a last look at Dublin because that's the last you'll see of it'.

She never mentions to the neighbours that she is from Dublin, they regard the Southern Irish as collaborators: and her with four boys fighting for the country!

She asks Pa if he is going to Midnight Mass. He is filling in his football coupon. His glasses have a mend in the middle with a plaster wrapped round where his nose goes. His eyes are screwed together trying to fit the eight zeros in eight small squares to forecast the eight draws which will bring a fortune. Alice knows he has a flutter on the horses and he does his coupon religiously. She never knew she had married a gambling man. But they had been well provided for, better if he had not consumed so much whisky.

She wishes he would fix his glasses, but he never listens to what she says. Passers-by brought him home last week after he bumped into a tram. She says a prayer to Saint Theresa every time he goes out now. He will be going out soon to do his spotting on the school roof but she suspects he just goes to make the tea. There is no way he could spot an enemy aircraft even if it hit him, just like the tram.

Alice picks up the dishes and puts them in the sink whilst Pa stretches out and reaches for his pipe again. Occasionally he puts some slack on the fire from the scuttle on the hearth. Pa calls it division of labour.

'That's the last of it today,' she tells him. 'The coal I mean. I've put some by for Christmas day.'

Alice reaches Pa's tin hat from the peg and hands

it to him as he leaves for his Air Raid Precaution duties, she sits by the dying fire and picks up the rug which is half finished. As she pegs away, she has a wish list for Christmas. In truth it is nothing from the shops, nothing flashy. Her list is really made up of things no longer there. First her boys. What would it be like to have them home and the table full again with the shouting and the arguments as they play cards? There would be no telling off about the language if only they could be here. And what would it be like to go to the butchers and order a leg of lamb and a string of sausages?

'How about six oranges and a couple of bananas?' she would say to the greengrocer. And they would be handed over without the palaver which happens now. 'Sorry madam, unless you have a green ration book - these are reserved for pregnant women.' She sighs and rolls up the rug. Better dust off her coat with the fur collar for Midnight mass. It would be nice to have a white Christmas but then she would worry if her shoes would survive another year. She is convinced her last pair were mainly cardboard. There are no coupons left to replace them if Pa is to have a new overcoat.

Alice removes the iron sheet from the massive range and covers it before slipping it into bed. She does not regret the lack of hot water bottles. They went out with the incoming war: rubber was more preciously placed on trucks and tanks. No, no regrets for the hot water bottles, the Iron sheet will still be warm when Pa returns from duty.

So many problems! and Saint Theresa cannot solve all, but she has a word before turning in, it makes her feel better.

16

FAMILIAR FEUDING

Simeon looked through the glass panel and could see a blurred outline of the gang of cousins he called his relations. The murmur coming from the room was as indistinct as the blurred outline. The hum was distinctly human, not be mistaken for the noise coming from the generator in the bowels of this old building. He stood for a moment, as a writer he wanted to pinpoint the sound, then he got it, it reminded him of those old movies where a telephone exchange processes messages and above the buzz you hear nothing important except the enticing,

'I'm putting you through'.

'Well,' he thought, 'I'd better put myself through and find out exactly what's being said. I know it will start with *why did you kill our grandfather*?

A row of faces: Cousin Arthur, the solicitor florid in pinstripe, wrinkled Alice his downtrodden wife in uncrushable polyester, Cousin Cissy, always abroad,

117

well toasted and approaching prune status, Marigold, grandfather's buxom, blithe and debonair mistress and Joanne. Nobody had met Joanne till today. Old Joe's only child from a previous marriage. She looked fruity, with her Blackberry eyes and raspberry lips opening on to those undeniably American teeth. She had mahogany hair in a stylish bob, and she'd come from New York.

'Well, you've kept us waiting long enough young man, what have you got to say for yourself?' Arthur boomed.

'What do you want to know?' he asked.

'You know very well why we're gathered here. You're in trouble mister and we want some answers before Bingham comes to read the will'.

'Hold on, Marigold interposed, can we start again and keep the volume down.'

They all turned to her, disdain in their expressions which said it all. *Who are you, the mistress, to interfere in a serious family discussion about why Old Joe's gone and where his money's going? he* could only repeat,

'What do you want to know? And why am I in trouble?' Arthur, the self-appointed legal spokesman demanded, 'We all want to know why grandfather, Old Joe, was taken to Switzerland, to that place,' he almost spat, 'without the family's permission.'

'I'm family', Simeon reminded them, 'and he didn't ask for the wider family to be consulted especially when he hadn't seen any of you for,' he paused looking around the group. to allow them to gather their wits. 'Arthur30 years, Cissy 40, Joanne 20?'

Cissy suddenly found her voice,

'Simeon you're the youngest cousin, I don't really think you should have taken a decision like that without talking to someone'.

'There was no-one there except Marigold and between us he was cared for, loved, entertained, ultimately obeyed. What more can I say? It was his wish.'

'Is it in writing?' Arthur asked suspiciously. He

handed over grandfather's letter together with all the paraphernalia attached to the business of allowing someone to die when they want to.

'Read the letter Arthur.' It was wrinkled Alice 's turn to comment.

'Just a minute, don't rush this.' Arthur scowled at Alice. That was a ticking off for the interruption. Winded, Alice retired to her corner and never uttered another word. 'We want to know what part Simeon here played in putting him up to this.'

'Read the letter.' Joanne commanded.

That startled everyone as Joanne had remained quiet throughout the conversation. The cousins were getting their first proper look at her. They knew **of** her of course, in between letters to borrow money and the odd phone call to Old Joe, the information had come their way. Now they were taking in the fact that Joanne was his daughter. She was his first wife Judith's kid, lived in the States and never been seen before today.

'Joanne dear.' Cissy started.

'I said read it.' Joanne commanded. In the American accent she had acquired living most of her life in New York, the tone of voice said *cut the crap and move on.* Simeon was on the same wavelength as Joanne. But he saw no point in Arthur toiling through Old Joe's papers. He fed on paper and his enjoyment would be prolonged chewing over every morsel.

'You can read his letter afterwards, but I can give you a precis,' he interrupted, 'Old Joe had simply had enough. He made his fortune in boxes, this shape, that shape, just like pallets which are needed everywhere to stack things, nothing happens without a box of sorts.'

'We know how his money was made.' Arthur said irritably.

'It's relevant,' he continued, 'he'd made a lot of money and there was no challenge in making more boxes, more money. He'd helped all of you at some stage in your lives, duty fulfilled. He'd lost all his sisters, (our mothers) and his closest blood relation Joanne lived abroad, end of family. His letter tells you that I lived

121

with him for support whilst I established myself as a writer, but he will tell you also that he enjoyed the journey with me. Now he was weary, and the weariness added up to a lack of interest in going on. He was not ill, just dead to the world. It happens.'

'That sounds like words put into his mouth by someone who monkeys with them.' Arthur stuttered, 'What do you write?'

'Detective stories.' he replied aware he was feeding Arthur the next line.

'You see.' Arthur exploded, 'He knows all about plots and ways round the police. But I think we should pass this over to them to investigate any funny business.' It took the wind out of Arthur's sails when Simeon added,

'I haven't finished yet. I know how Old Joe has left his money and I can assure you there's nothing there for me. He put me on my feet and said *now stand up*. And I did. If I've nothing to gain you don't have much of a case to go running to any authority with a complaint.' Arthur huffed and puffed a while before he decided to bully the group into asking the police to investigate Old Joe's suicide.

'I've come with a document here.' His lawyer's gimlet stare swept the group, 'We can all sign it before Bingham comes in to read the will. We need to clear the air around Simeon here. Family is family and I expect you all to sign up to an investigation.'

The group might have anticipated an objection from Marigold, but it was Joanne who spoke up.

'An investigation of Simeon, not in my name.' she twanged. 'None of us have any right to question what Simeon did, we were absent for most of Old Joe's life.'

'But life is life.' Well-travelled Cissy was sharing her wisdom.

'Just a reminder.' Joanne continued, it was *his* life, Old Joe's life. His decision which should be respected. Doctors ease you out of this life if you're in pain, I don't see you getting moral about that.'

'Oh my, they may do that in America,' Cissy argued, 'but he wasn't even ill.'

'Well, **I** get it,' she admonished them, 'he didn't need a dicky liver to give him a jaundiced view of this life, as Simeon said, he'd had enough.'

'We'll be having walk in clinics on the high street the way you're talking Joanne.' Further wisdom from Cissy.

'What a good idea,' she replied. 'Women can get rid of babies they don't want, they can control life, why can't old people oversee their lifespan?'

And so, it went on until Bingham arrived.

Nobody was very pleased with what Old Joe left them. Most of them had worked out his worth and their own percentage and it shocked them when most of it went to Marigold. Even Joanne missed out but took it with good grace. Simeon's only regret was that the old man hadn't seen Joanne, he might have lived for her.

Of course, none of them knew that he and Marigold were an item.

17

ON GOSSAMER WINGS

Summer is here. The shadows are sharp in the morning. They fall on the petunias I planted in May. A slight breeze lifts their petals. They are a very seductive chorus line singing 'Look at me'.

I make my way outside, a glass of cucumber gin in my hand. A warm breath of air lifts my long hair and I nod to the fluttering petunias, 'Lovely feel, isn't it?' I say. They make no reply of course. I'm sure they would like to, but they are busy fussing with two blue butterflies that make calls on each flower. I'm watching the butterflies with interest because I know the blues are males and they seem to be flirting with the browner females. Many of them won't live for long and they are frolicking in this unexpected breath of Summer: butterflies are like ticker tape celebrating its arrival. They have a summer of love just as we do.

Everyone has one surely. The time when you

first fall in love and the world leaps into colour. It's possibly the hormones but it just seems that way. My first love sat in front of me in church. His brown hair curled over his collar changing the shape of each curl as he turned his head. I learned his name and cunningly wrote his initials backward in my diary as a reference to him. A girl must have secrets. He was from over the tracks where rich people lived in detached houses. His invitation for a ride out to the bluebell woods was very polished followed by a shy 'yes' from me. From then on we spent the school holidays in the woods, boating on the lake and riding our cycles everywhere. The odd exchange of a kiss was not what it was about, then. Then it was just the pleasure of being together. He had more pocket money than me and we had two real dates going to the cinema. And then, he broke my heart simply by not turning up one day. Summer was over, the sun seemed to shut down, scent went out of the flowers, the woods turned menacing, and the boating lake was a place where you could drown. The cruelty of that

126

moment ruined the rest of the summer.

Wan Wan, my ginger cat, is just as attentive to the garden as I am. He's sitting under the Big Acer which throws the prettiest, lacy shade. If you didn't know him, you would think he was dozing: his eyes are narrowed to slits. A long time ago I understood his plans and belled his bright red collar. Now, try as he does, he will never stop the singing of a single bird. They are all round me celebrating the summer also. Wan Wan has been the name of a generation of cats I owned. They spell Nigel Alexander Wright backwards.

A drift of heavenly scent comes over from the sweet marjoram tumbling down the rocks surrounding a herb area. That is where you can crush the sharp lemon balm and bruise the bitter thyme leaves through your fingers. Green is my favourite colour so that little island shows all shades from the sludge green of mint to the luminant basil leaves. The ice at the bottom of my glass tinkles as I walk. My garden is in the national guide to private gardens which are opened to visitors. I'm expecting a group of six who will look round the garden and pay a small fee as they leave. Gardening is my 'thing' and each May to June, I open it up to the public, keep a pot for donations and give the takings to charity. I am a very young widow, and this is my solace. I have already laid out biscuits and cool drinks in the conservatory. I look forward to my group of visitors but showing the garden has been a steep learning experience, hence the gin, just in case.

I have had to ban dogs since one woman let her hound loose and he dug up the patch of irises. She was followed by one enthusiast who helped herself generously as she trailed behind everyone on her journey round the garden. I only spotted the basket full of Verbena as she was leaving. Who would do that? Usually, people are appreciative and interested. They have gardens of their own and love what my big one offers: except for a Mrs Trench, a lady who lectured me all round the tour pointing out what should have been the botanical names for the bushes and flowers. I speak to my plants with their common names Escallonia, Rock Rose, Lythodermas and label them accordingly. She was not pleased and left without a donation.

I look at my watch and see there's still ten minutes before the group arrives. The butterflies are still flirting, dancing around as if played in by James Galway's flute. The piece Tambourin has them leaping to his crescendos and they are joined with some painted ladies from Africa who are very acrobatic.

This garden is mine. I qualified as a botanist. My husband Herbert was a banker and worked late and long hours, so it was never a mutual pleasure. In fact, the letter 'B' of our trades was the only thing we shared. However, he never grudged the money which turned that patch over there into gold of another kind: African marigolds with fat sunny heads. A little unsteady now, I make my way into the kitchen to return my empty glass. I stumble past the waxen lilies, stunning and upright in a box. Oh dear, only just now I notice it looks like a coffin. That was unintended but, they do magnificently in their confined space. They are an exclusive bloom: very regal. Those same lilies were on Herbert's grave last summer. I ask myself the question which recurs from time to time, 'do I want another Herbert in my life?' The honest answer is, Herbert was a mistake. Mine was not a happy marriage. I still harbour dreams, but not of a 'Herbert'. And one never knows. Fate can be as fickle as the climate. I look up at the sky: the blue of forget- me- nots, 'sorry Mrs Trench, myosotis's.

And the guests are here. Five of them. I expected six. After introductions about toilets and refreshments I turn to see, presumably number six of the party, disappearing down the path to the Rhododendrons. The group follows me as I follow him. Close up, a shiver runs through me as I see curls sneak out of his collar at the back.

'Excuse me,' I call. He turns to face the group. 'Are you a member of the party here?'

'Indeed.' He replies. 'Am I doing something wrong? This is the Appleton Garden?'

'It is,' I assure him.' You just missed the intro about toilets and nibbles in the conservatory. So I Just wanted to fill you in. Please carry on. Everyone is free to wander. I keep up just to make sure no-one misses the best bits.' We are now staring at each other, snake and mouse, transfixed mode. The group senses something which is not their concern and slowly melts away. On auto pilot I call, 'I'll catch you up.'

'Why did you not turn up?' I ask. There is no need to explain the question, we are both back to age 16.

'I was sent away to boarding school.' Suddenly the tilted world rights itself. Of course. That's just what parents in his superior neighbourhood did. 'And when I looked you up, you were away at university. What are you?'

'A botanist. And you?'

'I'm a scout for film locations. Down here in Dorset because they're doing something on Hardy.'

The silence fills with buzzing and chirruping in the wild grasses. Insects and little animals are busy in the undergrowth of my wild patch. A biplane echoes the droning, dipping into the fleecy clouds. The silence is not awkward, It is just an interval as we take in the moment and a tune, an Adele love song, plays in my head.

The cat suddenly makes a leap up the Acer and falls back with a yelp.

'Wan Wan,' I admonish, 'Let the birdies live.'

'He doesn't look Siamese or Eastern in any way. In fact, he's a real British moggy. What's with the name?'

I ignore the question. He is already looking thoughtful. It wasn't a Bletchley Park kind of code after all. I knew he would work it out. Then? A painted lady, all the way from Africa lands on his shoulder. With a proprietary gesture I brush it away gently.

'That's a genus Cynthia. One of the strongest signals summer is here.'

'Let's hope it stays.' He replies. I can see he has solved the Nigel Alexander Wright code.

18

PET CHRISTMAS

Yes, this is different. I'm a dog. My name is 'Spot' after my nose I suppose as I'm sand-coloured everywhere else. I am a member of Potter's pack at number 22 Forest Gardens and top dog is Mr Potter who is also a fireman. I should correct that, top dog is the cat Gypsy who rules the chairs, the radiators and the snug from which I am banned.

The Potters are preparing for Christmas, and they are giving me a hard time. I have never been so vilified.

Spot you're a menace. Get yourself outside you're under my feet again.

You're asking for it Spot, get out the way. How would you like to be put down?

It's the season of goodwill Spot but it's fast running out, buzz off.

So, I did, I went outside.

I have a mate next door and we chat in the gaps of the hornbeam hedge. I'm pleased to say, the mate, Digger, is suffering too. He's been kicked out because he ran off with some streamers. He claims he was only joining in the fun which defines Christmas. We come together sharing our sorrows but really Digger is a menace at other times. He is a born thief. He wriggles through the hedge and digs up my bones and carries them off to his patch. He's a Terrier, so what can you expect? – No pedigree, unprincipled.

After I've had a moan, I decide to go inside as it's getting chilly. Ha! Gypsy has got the rug in front of the fire again but, what a treat: they have erected a tree just for me. Last year and every other year, we had a small plastic one that sat on the piano; this time they are obviously saying "sorry" for recent abuse and there's my tree, a real one.

'Oh, thank you.' I say and move over to have a sniff. No other dogs have been here, it's all mine. I promptly mark out my territory with a great arch of the leg. 'Look Gypsy, my tree. Have at you Moggy.'

And then the roof falls in.

'Mum, Spot's peeing on the tree.'

I am kicked outside again. My mate, Digger, is out again too. He's stolen some ham. I mentioned his failings, didn't I?

I'm called in for dinner but my tail droops in sadness.

'Cheer up Spot, it's Christmas. You've only yourself to blame for being kicked out.'

This is not a peace treaty. Humiliation is piled on as I see them set up the dog cage in the corner. That means the family with the squawking kids is coming. The children are such wallies: they belong to city folk who see the animal kingdom as packaged beef in the supermarket and dogs only on the Telly. Fine animals like me are anathema. The children took one look at me two years ago and let out hysterical screams. I was incarcerated for the remainder of their visit. To add to the misery, the kids fought over picking up Gypsy and stroking her whilst she looked at me with her evil, slitty eyes. 'Don't you wish you were me?'

'Wait till they get to know you, alley cat,' I signalled back. But I know this is a pipe dream; she has them fooled.

After dinner, they forget my cigar, to be precise, a chicken chew. I retire, squashed and defeated, to the cage. Ironically, they hold the door open and invite me in as if it's the bridal suite at the Ritz.

'Come on, Spotty dog. It's only pro-tem, and we're not locking you in.'

'Yes,' I'm thinking, 'that will change when the Squawkers arrive.'

*****

The next morning I'm free to depart my mini prison to get my breakfast, exiting with head high and dignity. I hope they understand how bruised my ego is.

It is now apparent that the dog tree was never, ever that. The Potter children are hanging bells on it and winding its branches with sparkling streamers. The

Squawker family has not arrived yet so I still have free run of the house and I watch as lights go on the tree and presents are piled at its feet where outside trees have weeds and grass. I see one box labelled 'Spot' and another labelled 'Gypsy' but the big mystery is one called 'Fifi'. I pop outside to discuss the development with Digger, my mate. Fifi is not a human name; it suggests another animal. Digger agrees and suggests a rabbit. He's a bit stupid sometimes. I remind him that we've got rabbits and Mr Potter threatens to shoot them with his air gun if he catches them eating his lettuce.

'Then it could be a gerbil.' Digger is obsessed with Gerbils. Digger's pack has got one that looks like a rat and Digger has an emotional meltdown with the urge to eat it.

'Maybe it's a donkey,' he volunteers. His ideas are getting dafter, so I wind up my visit.

'Let me know what happens,' is his parting shot. 'I bet it's another dog. That'll put your nose out of joint wont it pal?' I don't know why I speak to Digger sometimes he's so ignorant.

It's the day before the guests arrive and apart from the snug, I can still roam. I'm getting excited with all the smells that come from this Christmas celebration. It's quite intoxicating. Although I'm not a fan of the sweet stuff, I get enthusiastic with the children as they help with the pudding. They all have to have a stir for luck and they put money in. Amazing. Around the table is a forest of legs and me, we're all mixed up and happy, jostling for position. This is my kind of game.

Mrs Potter brings out a goose. That's a new one on me, we usually have turkey. Either or, my nose is triggered and when the pork comes out it goes to DEFCON 1. This part of Christmas is OK by me and I retire dreaming of 'goose'- combinations, permutations.

It's Christmas morning and the Squawker family has arrived. The grown-ups are the first to enter and everyone is circling then getting up close, probably smelling each other in a friendly way. Then, enter my nemesis, the two Squawker children. Without being told

I retreat to the cage. The CD player has been going from early morning with jingles and bells and as they enter there's a great crescendo 'Hallelujah'. How did the music know the moment? The Squawker kids are carrying a puppy, same nationality as myself, a Labrador. There is no need to eavesdrop as the following conversations are carried out in loud squeals.

'A darling – what's her name? How old? Where did you get?

'I thought the kids were scared of dogs.'

'They were. We thought that was nonsense and decided to introduce them to a dog.'

'For life I hope, brother?'

'Of course, big sister. I know we're city folks but we do have parks and walks by the canal. So, two birds with one stone, the kids get the dog and learn to take care of it AND it gets them out of the house.'

My heart soars, so this is the' Fifi' on the label

She is put in the cage with me, for her own good. I don't mind the cage now at all. I fill her in about the house rules: we are not allowed to be fed from the table, but I indicate where the best places are to station yourself for falling scraps. I tell her about Digger but most of all I tell her about Gypsy. I am elated that we are two dogs to one cat and ecstatic to see that Gypsy is now ignored by the two Squawker children. She has gone off to sulk in the snug.

This has been the worst anticipated Christmas but has turned out the best ever. Around the dinner table Big Sister, Mrs Potter, went on at length about 'a dog is not just for Christmas, it's for life'. But, apart from the odd scraps of pork that fell between myself and Fifi (stationed where I told her) were the tasty bits about myself.

'You'll see, when Fifi gets bigger, she'll be a lovely friendly pet, like our Spot.'

And Mr Potter, 'Yes, he's part of the family, we can't think of the Potters without a Spot Potter.' That's a good tongue twister, he says. They all have a try saying my name and pack name and fall about laughing. The uninhibited body movements direct a few bits of 'goose' our way. A bit fatty but, very acceptable, me and Fifi decide. It's nice to have these discussions with the same nationality.

When they pulled the crackers there was more hilarity. It seemed each joke sent tastier scraps to me and Fifi. We eat so much I don't think I can face my usual dinner.

Presents were handed out after lunch. There were lots more squeals and sniffing hugs between the Potters and the Squawkers then Fifi and I are out to play with our own presents. Mine was the one that throws a ball from a sling, you never know which direction it's going. Then, you retrieve it, lay it at someone's feet and, off we go again. It's like a conversation with your team.

'Throw it – Wait – fetch it- good dog – throw it again, different place please – there you go – thanks – clever boy.'

Digger is watching through the hornbeam hedge. I nudge Fifi who has been given a toy which gives out a very rude noise when she tries to bite it. Digger has his eye on it.

By the time our dinner is served, Fifi and I, as predicted, can hardly finish it. We retire to the cage, Fifi cuddled up to me and we sleep. Both packs were similarly prone with overeating and lolled around the T V, probably all afternoon.

*****

It was sad when leaving time came for the Squawkers.

'We should get together more often,' were the sentiments. 'Why only at Christmas?'

My feelings exactly. When Fifi comes next year (I hope) I will be training her up as a terrorist to assault Gypsy.

END

About the Author

Barbara grew up and was educated in Sheffield, England. She married an Indian national and moved to India, where she lived for 15 years while also pursuing further education. She returned to the UK in 1970 and worked as a civil servant. On retirement, she was a volunteer in the education part of the National Trust at Chirk Castle for 10 years. In between, she did a five-year tour of places in Shropshire, delivering talks on Indian life. Barbara has a wry take on human behaviour which has produced this second set of short stories to entertain. The author has always written, paid or unpaid and has published a novel on India, as well as a mystery romance and two books of short stories. At almost 92 she continues her love with words and their power to expose the world to the reader. This habit of a 92-year lifetime, observing and writing about people, continues. After all there are 8 billion people on this earth. Way to go.

Milton Keynes UK
Ingram Content Group UK Ltd.
UKHW042140170324
439575UK00001B/3